ABRACADABRA!

Original title: *Prova a dire Abracadabra!*

© Camelozampa, Italy, 2017

Published by
MAGINATION PRESS ®
American Psychological Association
750 First Street NE
Washington, DC 20002

Magination Press is a registered trademark of the American Psychological Association.

For more information about our books, including a complete catalog, please write to us, call 1-800-374-2721, or visit our website at www.apa.org/pubs/magination.

English translation by Katie ten Hagen
Book design by Susan K. White
Printed by Lake Book Manufacturing, Inc.

Library of Congress Cataloging-in-Publication Data
Names: Giraldo, Maria Loretta, author. | Bertelle, Nicoletta, illustrator. | ten Hagen, Katie, translator.
Title: Abracadabra! : the magic of trying / by Maria Loretta Giraldo ; illustrated by Nicoletta Bertelle ; English translation by Katie ten Hagen. Other titles: Prova a dire abracadabra!
English Description: Washington, DC : Magination Press, [2018] | "American Psychological Association." | "Original title Prova a dire Abracadabra! Camelozampa, Italy 2017"—Title page verso. | Summary: Little Owl is afraid of falling and will not try to fly until his forest friends persuade him to say a special word—and keep trying, even after he fails. Includes note for parents.
Identifiers: LCCN 2017039828| ISBN 9781433828744 | ISBN 143382874X
Subjects: | CYAC: Persistence—Fiction. | Owls—Fiction. | Flight.
Classification: LCC PZ7.1.G5825 Abr 2018 | DDC [E]—dc23 LC record available at https://lccn.loc.gov/2017039828

Manufactured in the United States of America
10 9 8 7 6 5 4 3 2 1

ABRACADABRA!
THE MAGIC OF TRYING

by Maria Loretta Giraldo
illustrated by Nicoletta Bertelle

MAGINATION PRESS ● **WASHINGTON, DC**
American Psychological Association

Today was an important day at
the little birds' school.
Today was the day they all learned how to fly!
They jumped off the branch,
opened their wings, and…**flew!**

The first was Blackbird. He launched himself
into the air and yelled, "Hooray! How fun!"
Next came Robin. "Yippee! How fun!"
Then it was up to Sparrow. "Yay! How fun!"
And then Canary, Swallow, and Hummingbird.

Little Owl opened his wings. "Abicidabra!" he said, and jumped. And…**CRASH!** He fell down.

"Ouch, ouch," cried Little Owl. "You see? Your word doesn't work."

"Wait," responded Turtle. "Make sure to say **ABRA-CA-DABRA!** Go on, try again."

Just then Mouse, who had been listening, came along.
"What's going on?" he asked.
"Little Owl is afraid of flying," explained Turtle.
"Nonsense!" said Mouse. "Did you tell him to say
ABRACADABRA? That might help."

Little Owl shook his head.
"It doesn't work. I just said it and I still fell."
"Try again!" insisted Turtle.

Little Owl went back up the tree and tried again.
He closed his eyes and said "abracadabra."
He flew a little bit, a little bit more. Here and there, and then…
CRASH!
"Ouch ouch! But this time I said it right!"
"Yes, but you had your eyes closed," Mouse told him.
"Try again, and keep your eyes open. Imagine yourself flying.
Believe you can do it!"

Little Owl went back up the tree, opened his eyes as big as he could, and flapped his wings. "Abracadabra," he said.
He went up high, a little, a little more, still a little more.
But then…**CRASH!**
"Ouch ouch ouch!" he cried desperately.

Meanwhile, Hedgehog had arrived. "What's going on?" he asked.
"Little Owl cannot fly," Mouse and Turtle told him.

"Oh. Just say ABRACADABRA and you will fly for sure!" said Hedgehog.
"I have tried that so many times, and still, look! Every time, I fall."
"But maybe you said it too softly. Try to say it with all the breath that
you have in your chest! And concentrate," insisted Hedgehog.

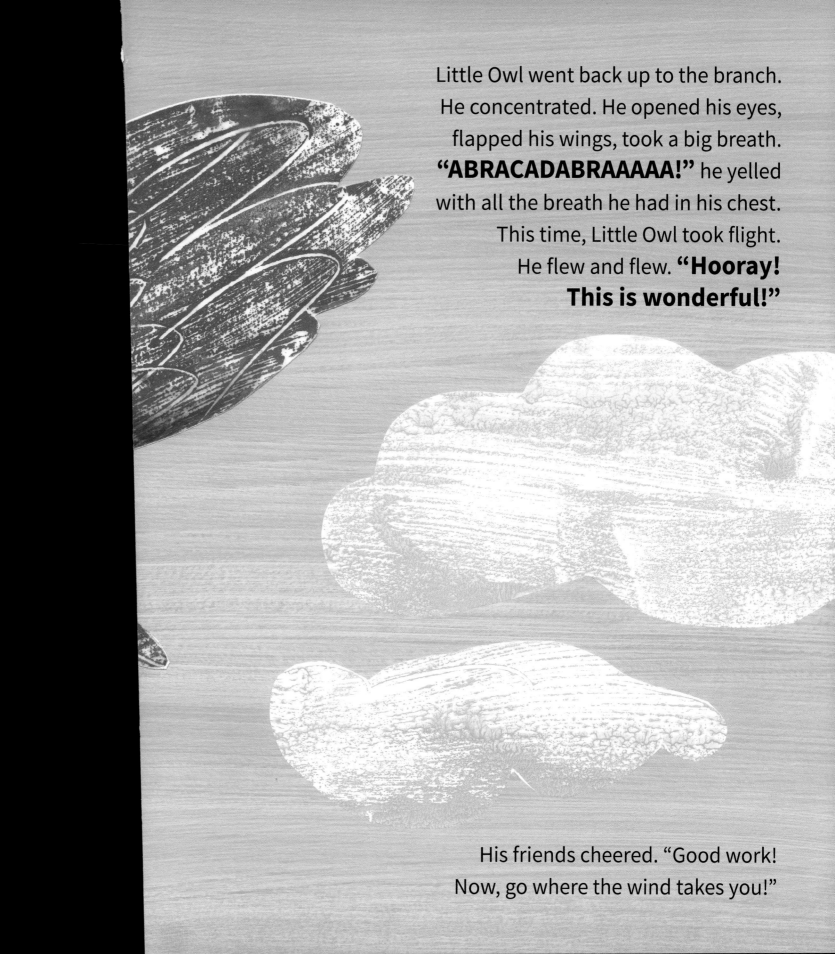

Little Owl went back up to the branch.
He concentrated. He opened his eyes,
flapped his wings, took a big breath.
"ABRACADABRAAAAA!" he yelled
with all the breath he had in his chest.
This time, Little Owl took flight.
He flew and flew. **"Hooray!**
This is wonderful!"

His friends cheered. "Good work!
Now, go where the wind takes you!"

The wind took him over the pond, where there was a
school for little frogs. Today was a very important day for
the frogs: For the first time, they had to leave the pond,
making a great big jump up to the shore.

The first frog tried, and…**HOP**!
The second frog tried, and…**HOP**!
Then the third, and the fourth, and the fifth…
HOP, HOP, HOP!
Finally, almost all the frogs had made it to the shore.
Only one remained in the pond.
Little Frog was sad. She didn't want to make the big jump.

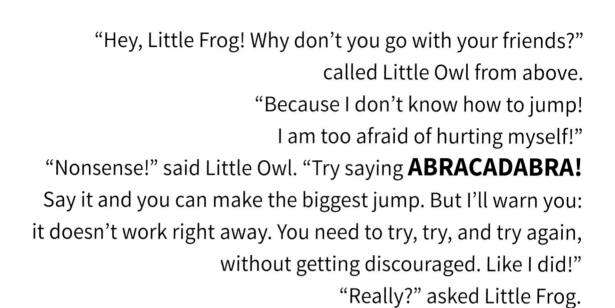

"Hey, Little Frog! Why don't you go with your friends?"
called Little Owl from above.
"Because I don't know how to jump!
I am too afraid of hurting myself!"
"Nonsense!" said Little Owl. "Try saying **ABRACADABRA!**
Say it and you can make the biggest jump. But I'll warn you:
it doesn't work right away. You need to try, try, and try again,
without getting discouraged. Like I did!"
"Really?" asked Little Frog.
"For sure!"

Note to Parents and Caregivers

by Ara J. Schmitt, PhD

"If at first you don't succeed, try, try again" is a familiar quote that was popularized by William Edward Hickson. These words invoke the notion that hard work and perseverance produce positive results for children and adults! So important is this notion that the U.S. Department of Education produced a 2013 report entitled *Promoting Grit, Tenacity, and Perseverance: Critical Factors for Success in the 21st Century*. The report says that perseverance, or the ability to accomplish goals in the face of challenges and setbacks, requires a certain mindset and tools specific to the task at hand. These ideas are used as the basis of this note.

How to Use This Book

Little Owl in *Abracadabra!* was faced with the challenge of learning how to fly, and certainly faced setbacks along the way. After all, it took the support of four others, working through multiple crashes, and a *seemingly* magical term for him to finally get it! *Abracadabra!* works to normalize the idea that practice, perseverance in the face of setbacks, and often even the support of others are needed to reach important goals. This book is particularly useful for anyone who wants to promote perseverance as a necessary life skill, support a child who is experiencing frustration as a result of setbacks, or even reassure a child hesitant to try unfamiliar tasks out of fear of failure. Is magic required, as the term "abracadabra" might imply? Of course not. The phrase merely prompted Little Owl to practice flying—again and again!

Setting the Stage for Perseverance

The development of perseverance is complex and unique to each child. The child's environment, opportunity to take on new challenges, and the presence of an encouraging support system all play a role. The development of perseverance is aided by three key psychological concepts: strategies, self-control, and a growth-oriented mindset. These concepts are crucial whether the challenge is posed by a classroom teacher, an athletic coach, a music instructor, or you!

Strategies

It may seem obvious to us, but developing a plan to solve a problem is a key skill that must be taught to a child. A child must understand the task to be accomplished, develop a plan to reach the goal, monitor how they are doing, and figure out how to change their approach if it isn't working. So, how can a parent help?

- *Ensure understanding of the goal.* One way to check your child's understanding is to have your child state their understanding of the goal in their own words. If the ultimate goal is not well understood, undue frustration may result.
- *Identify steps.* Most complex tasks require several steps, and time to accomplish. Teach your child to identify the steps that will lead to mastery of a task and establish mini-goals so that the child feels a sense of accomplishment along the way. If a child can see progress, they are more likely to persevere. Little Owl had to take a deep breath, flap his wings, and, most importantly, *believe!* (Early on, when he doubted himself, he substituted belief in a word for belief in himself, but by the end he realizes that it was all him.)
- *Provide support.* Children may need assistance monitoring how they are progressing. This may involve providing supportive examples of the child's progress towards a goal.
- *Reevaluate when necessary.* When a child is

stuck or not progressing, a parent may need to help them identify the specific strategies that were used that are not working, and what different strategies could be used to move forward. Emphasize that it is normal for the first idea or attempt to not work; it just means they have to try something new! Little Owl had to try many times and adjust what he was doing each time.

Self-Control

Most goals worth accomplishing take time to complete and, as discussed, take practice and fine-tuning of strategies to be successful. Self-control refers to the ability work through short-term issues in order to reach the longer-term goal. This means the ability to pay attention, ignore impulses, delay gratification, and manage one's own emotional responses. Of course, this can be difficult with a child, especially in the beginning! But there are many ways parents can help their children work on their self-control.

- *Foster attention.* Parents may help their child sustain attention by creating a distraction-free (or as close as possible) environment for their child to work or practice in. Chunking a task into easier-to-manage parts and setting reasonable short-term goals can also help keep a child focused. Finally, providing a child a small reward (like a treat or a play break) for engaging in a short period of hard work or accomplishing a short-term goal can be very helpful. No one likes to work for free!
- *Manage impulses.* Poor impulse control may result in children being drawn to distracting objects and preferred activities, like playing video games, rather than to the task at hand. Removing distractions from the area in which a child is working or practicing

may help reduce impulsivity. Children with poor impulse control may also respond too quickly when completing a task, resulting in counterproductive mistakes. Parents can prompt the child to slow down or think carefully before responding.
- *Monitor emotions.* Any parent knows that children often need help managing their emotions! This is particularly true in the face of setbacks when learning a new skill. Making mistakes, recognizing when they occur, and correcting them is part of the learning process. You can point out how many times Little Owl wanted to give up because he was frustrated, but in the end he was glad that he pushed through.

Growth-Oriented Mindset

A *growth-oriented mindset* is when children believe that they can succeed, know that hard work is necessary, know that challenges and setbacks are part of the learning process and can be overcome, and eagerly look for new strategies to succeed. On the other hand, children with a *fixed mindset* consider a particular skill (or even intelligence!) to be an inborn trait that comes naturally to those who have it. As a result, children with a fixed mindset tend to not like effort, because applying effort is a sign that they are inherently not good at it. These children also tend to be overly discouraged by setbacks and are often defensive. Unsurprisingly, children with a growth-oriented mindset are more likely to be successful at learning new skills, whether mental or physical. Parents can help foster a growth-orientation by keeping the following things in mind:

- *Innate ability is rare!* Just like Little Owl learning to fly, almost every skill you can think of needs development. No one is born with the ability to read. It takes years of practice to learn how to fly an airplane. Even elite athletes readily admit that it takes a great deal of practice to succeed at a sport! Because social media is very much a part of children's lives, a parent might consider finding an internet clip of someone their child admires talking about the hard work they have put in. It might be encouraging for a child to hear someone like LeBron James or Adele talk about their journeys and practice habits.

- *Practice takes time!* Fast learning may not result in optimized performance. Learning proper techniques through repeated exposure takes time.
- *Focus on "challenges," rather than "successes."* Experts tell us that parents should praise children for their effort and the process of their learning rather than focusing on success. This allows the child to get a sense of achievement from progress, rather than constantly being disappointed by how long it is taking to reach the ultimate goal. This approach has long-term mental-health benefits in addition to promoting perseverance.
- *Practice a variety of challenges.* Although opportunities to complete long-term goals most naturally occur at school (e.g., academic goals and large projects), you might encourage your child to take on challenges at home. For example, your child might be encouraged to learn a new sport, learn a musical instrument, engage in a long-term art project, do a complex puzzle, or practice to participate in a competition of their choosing.
- *Mistakes are normal!* All of us have had to develop perseverance through challenges and setbacks. Reinforce to your child that mistakes are not bad, they are a normal part of learning. It could help to talk about a mistake you have made in the past, and what you did to move past it. This can be a truly bonding experience and help to normalize the feelings your child may have if a setback occurs or if a goal seems unreachable when it is very much possible.

Some children naturally persevere in the face of challenges, but most children learn the skills necessary to persevere through the loving support of caregivers. By fostering task-specific strategies, self-control, and a growth-oriented mindset, caregivers can help children become happy and successful adults!

Ara J. Schmitt, PhD, is an associate professor of school psychology at Duquesne University. His primary research interests involve the neuropsychological assessment and intervention of learning problems and pediatric disorders. Dr. Schmitt is also a licensed psychologist and certified school psychologist.

About the Author

MARIA LORETTA GIRALDO is an Italian children's writer based in Verona, Italy. She is the author of over 100 books published and translated all over the world. She works for publishers such as Giunti, Rizzoli, De Agostini, San Paolo, and many more. She is a long-term artistic partner of Nicoletta Bertelle.

About the Illustrator

NICOLETTA BERTELLE has illustrated more than 80 books for many Italian and foreign publishers. One of her books was chosen by Rai TV for a cartoon, and she was selected in 2002 for the White Ravens list. She is published by Giunti, San Paolo, Grimm Press, and many more. She lives in Padua, Italy.

About Magination Press

MAGINATION PRESS is an imprint of the American Psychological Association, the largest scientific and professional organization representing psychologists in the United States and the largest association of psychologists worldwide.